WELCOME TO
PASSPORT TO READING
A beginning reader's ticket to a brand-new world!

Every book in this program is designed to build read-along and read-alone skills, level by level, through engaging and enriching stories. As the reader turns each page, he or she will become more confident with new vocabulary, sight words, and comprehension.

These PASSPORT TO READING levels will help you choose the perfect book for every reader.

READING TOGETHER
Read short words in simple sentence structures together to begin a reader's journey.

READING OUT LOUD
Encourage developing readers to sound out words in more complex stories with simple vocabulary.

READING INDEPENDENTLY
Newly independent readers gain confidence reading more complex sentences with higher word counts.

READY TO READ MORE
Readers prepare for chapter books with fewer illustrations and longer paragraphs.

This book features sight words from the educator-supported Dolch Sight Words List. This encourages the reader to recognize commonly used vocabulary words, increasing reading speed and fluency.

For more information, please visit www.passporttoreadingbooks.com.

Enjoy the journey!

Little, Brown and Company

Hachette Book Group
237 Park Avenue, New York, NY 10017
Visit our website at www.lb-kids.com

Little, Brown and Company is a division of Hachette Book Group, Inc.
The Little, Brown name and logo are trademarks of Hachette Book Group, Inc.

The publisher is not responsible for websites (or their content) that are not owned by the publisher.

First Revised Edition: July 2013
First published in hardcover in July 2005 by Little, Brown and Company

ISBN 978-0-316-22931-9

10 9 8 7 6 5 4 3 2 1

IM

Printed in Malaysia

Book design by Saho Fujii

Passport to Reading titles are leveled by independent reviewers applying the standards developed by Irene Fountas and Gay Su Pinnell in Matching Books to Readers: Using Leveled Books in Guided Reading, Heinemann, 1999.

OTTO
Goes to School

Todd Parr

LITTLE, BROWN AND COMPANY
New York Boston

Wake up, Otto!
It is the first day of school!

Otto gets dressed.
He is so excited that
he puts his shirt on backward.
And he wears two
different socks.

Silly Otto!

He has his favorite breakfast:
cereal, juice, and a banana split.

"Yum!" says Otto.

HONK! HONK!
The bus is here.
Otto gets on.
He rides to school.

At school, Otto sees a red dog,
a blue dog, a big dog, and
a little dog.
He even sees a polka-dotted cat.

Otto is worried because
he does not know anyone.

Then Otto sees his friends
Cool Kitty and Noodle Poodle.
He feels better.

He meets his new teacher, too.

Otto learns all kinds
of new things.

He learns how to wag his tail
without knocking things over.

Good dog, Otto!

He learns that shoes
are for wearing,
NOT for eating.

Good dog, Otto!

He learns how to share his toys
and play games.

Good dog, Otto!

He learns it is not okay
to chase squirrels.

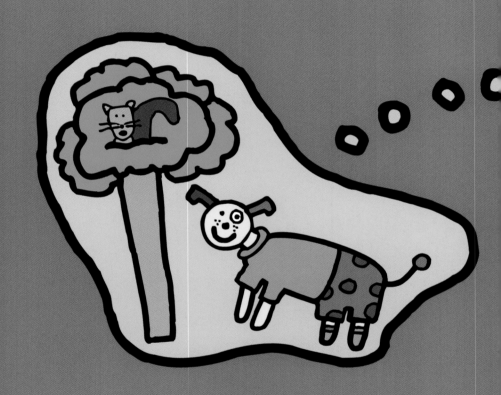

Good dog, Otto!

He learns to wait his turn
for the bathroom.

Good dog, Otto!

Otto loves the first day
of school.
He is so good that he gets
a special treat.

Otto even gets a blue ribbon.

On the way home,
Otto rolls in a puddle.
He gets mud all over
the house.

Oh no, Otto!

But Otto is not worried.
He has a whole school year
to learn more!

A note from Todd:

The first day of school
is fun and exciting.
You will make new friends
and learn new things,
and you will be really smart.

Love, Otto
and Todd